The Rescue Princesses

The Golden Shell

More amazing animal adventures!

The Rescue Princesses

The Golden Shell

♥ PAULA HARRISON ♥

Scholastic Inc.

In memory of Alf and Dorothy

ISBN 978-0-545-66168-3

Text copyright © 2014 by Paula Harrison
Interior illustrations copyright © 2014 by Artful Doodlers

12 11 10 9 8 7 6 5 4 3 2   15 16 17 18 19/0

Printed in the U.S.A.   40
First printing, August 2014

First Day of School

Princess Ella gazed out at the trees and hedges flashing past the car window. She linked her fingers together tightly and tried to ignore the fluttering feeling in her tummy. It wouldn't be long now. Soon they would reach the Royal Academy for Princesses, her new school!

Ella tucked her dark, wavy hair behind her tiara and smoothed the gray pleats of her new school uniform. She was trying not to think about missing home, especially her puppy, Sesame, with his beautiful brown eyes and soft little paws. But thinking about her new school didn't make her feel better, either. Her mom had told her that the school was enormous. What if she got lost trying to find her way around? What if none of the other girls wanted to talk to her? What if —

"Are you all right, Ella?" Her mom, Queen Jade, turned toward her. "You look a little pale. Do you feel sick?"

"No, I'm fine." Ella tried to smile.

"Really?" The queen frowned. "You don't *look* fine. Maybe we'd better stop for a minute." She leaned forward to speak to the royal driver. "Stop at the side of the road, please."

The car pulled over next to a hedge. Ella's dad, King George, quietly snored from the front passenger seat.

"Your father nodded off again," said the queen, opening the car door. "Out you go! You'll feel much better after some fresh air."

Ella climbed out onto a grassy hill dotted with purple flowers. They were on a narrow lane with tall hedges on both sides. The sun shone brightly and thin wisps of white cloud floated in the sky.

The queen climbed out of the car, holding on to her golden crown. "Ah, there's something wonderful about the air here!" she said, smiling. "It makes me feel very energetic! I remember when I used to go to school here, many years ago. One day we all went on a long walk through the fields and . . ." The queen continued talking but Ella didn't listen closely to the rest.

Her mom had been talking about the old days at school a lot. She'd talked about them while making Ella try on her new green-and-gray uniform. Then she'd talked some more while packing Ella's suitcase. Ella knew that her mom had loved going to the Royal Academy for Princesses. She just wasn't sure she was going to like it, too!

She breathed deeply. Her mom was right. The air did seem fresher here. She noticed a gap in the hedge a little farther along and went to look through it. Sheep were grazing on the other side. Ella stared at the view beyond the field and her heart beat faster. In the distance there was a towering red-stone castle, and the sparkling blue sea.

"Wow! That's a really big castle." Ella gazed at its tall, square turrets. It looked much more old-fashioned than their palace back home.

"There it is!" said her mom, joining her. "Harebell Castle — home to the Royal Academy for Princesses."

"That's Harebell Castle? I didn't know we were so close!" said Ella, surprised.

"Yes, we're almost there." The queen smiled. "Let's keep going. We should reach the school in a few minutes."

Ella glanced at Harebell Castle one more time before returning to the car. She still felt a little nervous, but now that she'd seen the castle, she wanted to know what it was like inside.

They drove through the castle gates ten minutes later. As the car swept along, Ella stared at the large statues next to the driveway that had been created from hedges. One was a boat with a tall mast next to the shape of a sailor looking through a telescope. Ella's favorite was a starfish standing up on two legs.

A tall, gray-haired lady was waiting for them at the front entrance. She greeted them as they got out of the car and shook their hands.

"Good afternoon," she said in a clear and calm voice. "I'm Miss Goldwin, the Headmistress of the Royal Academy for Princesses, and you must be Princess Petronella."

Ella winced. Petronella was her full name, but her mom and dad only used it when they were angry with her. "Can you call me Ella?" she asked hopefully.

Miss Goldwin nodded. "Very well, Princess Ella! I hope you all had a good journey. Please come in." She led them through a door with sea creatures carved into the wood. Ella traced a finger along the carving of an octopus's long tentacle.

The red-stone walls gave a warm feeling to the inside of the castle. Two long staircases rose upward at opposite ends of the hallway and met on a wide balcony. In the center of the balcony was a huge bronze-colored bell standing on a wooden pedestal.

Queen Jade looked around, beaming. "It's just like I remember — the pictures of famous pupils on the walls and the smell of chocolate cake. I had such a wonderful time here."

Miss Goldwin led them into a large room with many tables. "This is our dining hall. We have assemblies in here on Fridays and put on concerts and plays at the end of each term." She swept a speck of dust off a nearby table. "This school year began two weeks ago. You'll be sharing a room with three other girls who are also starting their first year."

A girl with short blond hair came in. "Did you want to see me, Miss Goldwin?" she asked with a curtsy.

"Yes, I did, Rosalind," replied the head teacher. "This is Ella, who will be taking the empty bunk bed in your room. Please show her where she'll be sleeping."

Rosalind nodded. "Yes, Miss Goldwin, and then maybe I should show her around the rest of the school?"

"An excellent idea!" Miss Goldwin turned to Ella. "Rosalind will be your guide today, and I'll get someone to bring your suitcase upstairs in a moment."

"Good-bye, darling." Queen Jade hugged Ella. "Have a lovely time. We'll send you postcards from everywhere we go on our royal tour."

"Bye, Mom. Bye, Dad." Ella hugged them both. "I'll see you soon!" She felt excitement fizzing inside her as she followed Rosalind out of the hall.

"Did you have a really long journey?" asked Rosalind.

"Yes, it took five days to sail here from the Island of Varras. I like being on the ocean, though." Ella stopped, suddenly shy.

Rosalind smiled. "Come on — I'll show you where we sleep!"

Ella hurried after her. She couldn't wait to see her new bunk bed and look all around the rest of the castle!

CHAPTER TWO

Seahorse Tower

Ella followed Rosalind across the entrance hall and up the grand staircase. "Are you new here, too?"

Rosalind nodded. "I started two weeks ago, at the beginning of the year. So did Lottie and Summer, the other girls in our room. We wondered who would come to take the last bunk bed."

"I should have arrived at the start of the year like you," explained Ella. "But my mom and dad couldn't bring me till now because they've been getting ready for their royal tour. They'll be visiting places for weeks and weeks."

The girls reached the balcony and Ella stared at the enormous bronze-colored bell.

"They ring the bell three times for each mealtime," said Rosalind, noticing where Ella was looking.

"A bell that big must be really loud," said Ella.

"It is!" Rosalind turned a corner and led them up another staircase. "The castle has four towers, where we sleep. We're in Seahorse Tower."

Ella noticed three more staircases leading off in different directions. "What are the other towers called?" she asked.

"As well as Seahorse there's Coral, Jellyfish, and Barnacle," Rosalind told her. "I wouldn't want to sleep in Barnacle.

Their tower always seems so cold. Anyway, here we are!"

She pushed open a door that was painted with a gigantic picture of a seahorse and decorated with shells. The corridor beyond was painted blue-green with wavy shapes along it. Ella almost felt as if she were underwater.

The bedroom was large, with bunk beds at both ends and plenty of closets. Two girls were perched together on a top bunk with their legs hanging over the edge. They were both wearing the Academy uniform and pretty tiaras. They looked up as Ella walked in.

A girl with curly red hair and sparkling green eyes jumped down from the bunk. "Hello, I'm Lottie! Are you the new girl?"

Ella smiled. "Yes, I'm Ella!"

"I'm Summer." The second girl climbed down from the bunk and pushed her

golden hair behind her ears. "I hope you don't mind having a bottom bunk. Lottie and I took the top ones when we arrived."

"No, I don't mind." Ella noticed the seahorse quilts on each of the beds. "Are there lots of bedrooms in Seahorse Tower?"

"Five," said Lottie. "It's the smallest tower, but the coziest one, too! We'll show you around the whole place. You have to see the stables. And you have to see the music room, and the garden, and the pet barn, too."

Ella's eyebrows rose. She was just about to ask what the pet barn was when Rosalind broke in. "It's *my* job to show her around, Lottie. Miss Goldwin asked me to do it!"

Lottie folded her arms. "All right! Don't get your tentacles in a tangle! We can all show her around together, can't we?"

Ella liked that idea. She was just wondering how to agree with Lottie without upsetting Rosalind when a brightly colored parrot flew in through the open window. The bird landed on Summer's shoulder, folded his blue wings, and looked beadily at Ella. He tilted his head and squawked.

"Shh, Kanga!" said Summer. "You're not supposed to be in here."

A door banged farther up the corridor.

"Quick, Summer!" said Rosalind. "That could be Molly checking up on us again."

Summer took the parrot to the window and he flew away again.

"Is he yours?" asked Ella. "He's very beautiful."

"Yes, he's mine," said Summer. "He's supposed to stay in the bird house, but he doesn't seem to like it down there. He's used to roaming free at home, and now there are all these rules."

The bedroom door swung open and an older girl marched in. Her pointed face was framed by thin dark hair. "Have you brought that bird inside again? I told you before: it's *not* allowed! Only cats and dogs are allowed up here."

"Do you mean Kanga the parrot, Molly?" asked Lottie. "There are no birds in here. Look — no birds at all!"

The older girl looked around, frowning. "Well, make sure you don't bring him up here. The rules say no birds!" She muttered something about new girls, then — with an extra glare at Ella — she closed the door.

Lottie sighed. "That's Molly," she told Ella. "She's one of the Seahorse Tower captains. There are four of them — all older girls — in charge of this tower."

"The other captains seem nice but Molly just wants to boss everyone around all the time," said Summer.

"You see! That's why we can't ask just anyone to join," said Rosalind. "Molly would be awful as part of the —" She stopped suddenly and glanced at Ella.

Ella noticed the other girls exchanging looks. What had Rosalind been about to say? *Ask everyone to join what?*

Summer coughed awkwardly. "So, what pet did you bring, Ella?"

"I . . ." Ella looked confused. "I didn't bring a pet. Is everyone allowed to have one?"

"Oh yes! Every princess brings an animal with them. That's what the pet barn is for," said Lottie in surprise. "As long as it's not something too difficult to look after. I mean, they wouldn't be happy if you brought an elephant or something. It would be way too big!"

"Did you all bring animals with you?" Ella twisted the sleeve of her school sweater.

"I brought Kanga, my parrot," explained Summer.

"I brought a little hamster named Fluff," said Rosalind.

"And I brought my pony, Strawberry," added Lottie. "I couldn't bear to be away from her for long. I love riding her."

"Oh," said Ella.

"Don't you have a pet that you wanted to bring?" asked Lottie.

Ella thought of her beautiful puppy, Sesame, whom she'd left at home in his doggie bed. She swallowed. "No one said I was allowed to bring a pet. My mom told me a lot about coming to school here because she went here, too, a long time ago. But I guess they didn't have a pet barn back then."

Just then there was a knock at the door and a girl with two brown braids came in. "The mailman just arrived! Lottie and Summer, there are letters for you downstairs. Rosalind, I think you've got a package."

"Great!" Rosalind rushed to the door. "Do you want to stay here and settle in, Ella? We won't be long."

"Sure!" said Ella. "I'll wait here."

As they disappeared down the corridor, Ella heard Summer saying, "I think we should be careful who we tell about You Know What!"

Then the girls turned a corner and Ella couldn't hear any more. She pushed a lock of dark hair behind her ear. It seemed like there was something the other princesses didn't want her to know. Sighing, she walked over to the bedroom window.

Below her were the school playing fields. A tall fence marked the edge of the school grounds, and then the grass sloped down to a steep cliff. Beyond the cliff, the sea shimmered as sunlight danced on the waves. A handful of rocks jutted out of the water, guarded by a tall orange-and-white-striped lighthouse. For a moment Ella thought she could hear a faint song drifting on the wind.

She stared at the sea for a while. Somewhere beyond those waves was her home, but it was thousands of miles away. And now she'd found out she was going to be the only one in the whole school without a pet to play with.

"Ella? Are you all right?"

Ella swung around and saw that

Rosalind had come back in without her noticing. She took a deep breath and tried to smile.

"I came to get you! You need to come downstairs right away." Rosalind grabbed her hand. "Lottie and Summer and I have a surprise for you. I think you're going to like it!"

CHAPTER THREE

The Pet Barn

Ella raced along the corridor after Rosalind. They ran downstairs to the balcony with the bronze bell. Rosalind began pointing things out as they passed. "The music and art rooms are down that corridor," she said breathlessly. "And the staff room's there, too."

They carried on down the next set of stairs to the entrance hall.

"I promise I'll show you around the right way later on," added Rosalind.

"There's the dining hall — you've seen that, haven't you?"

Ella nodded. "Where do we go for classes?"

"There are lots of classrooms and a science lab around here somewhere," said Rosalind, waving her arm. "I get a little lost sometimes because there are so many rooms. That door with the purple crown painted on it is the Throne Room, where we have our Royal Skills classes."

Ella glanced curiously at the door with the purple crown. Her mom had told her a lot about the Royal Skills classes. Those were the lessons where you practiced behaving in a royal manner — learning to bow and curtsy.

"Come on! We can look at all that later." Rosalind pulled her out of the front door and they ran across the lawn together.

"Where are we going?" asked Ella.

Rosalind grinned. "You'll see!"

They ran past a row of greenhouses. Then Ella saw Lottie and Summer waving at them from the doorway of a long wooden barn.

"This is so exciting!" called Lottie. "I wish I was getting one, too!"

Ella's brow wrinkled. "What do you mean? Getting what?"

Summer giggled and stood back from the doorway. "Come inside and we'll show you."

Ella stepped into the shadowy barn. At first she couldn't see much. What was that smell? It made her think of hay and animals.

Rosalind switched on a light. "Welcome to the pet barn!"

"Oh!" Ella stared around the barn in delight. There were stalls on one side and rows of smaller hutches on the other.

A lamb bleated right next to her, making her jump. The little animal stuck its head over the side of its stall and looked at her nosily.

"What do you think?" said Rosalind, beaming.

"Wow! This is great!" said Ella. "I've never seen so many animals in one place."

"There are guinea pigs, gerbils, and hamsters here, as well as the sheep and chickens that belong to the school," explained Lottie. "Cats and dogs are allowed upstairs in the bedrooms as long as they're well behaved, and ponies, like my Strawberry, live in the stables."

"Birds live in the bird house next door, and that's where my parrot, Kanga, is supposed to be," said Summer. "Except that he keeps on escaping to come find me!"

"Hello, girls!" A lady with freckled

cheeks wearing jeans and boots came into the barn. "Ah, is this someone new?" She smiled at Ella.

"I'm Ella," said Ella shyly. "I arrived today."

"Nice to meet you!" the lady replied, brushing mud off her hands. "I'm Rebecca. I look after the pet barn and make sure that all the animals are happy and well cared for. Did you bring a pet with you?"

Ella shook her head sadly.

"But that's the good news!" Rosalind burst out. "We told Miss Goldwin that you don't have a pet, and she said you could choose one of the new baby rabbits!"

"Really?" asked Ella.

"Yes, really!" said Rosalind, grinning.

Ella's heart lifted. "Oh, thanks! That's amazing!"

"It was Rosalind's idea," said Lottie.

"Then Summer found Miss Goldwin and I asked her if it was okay."

"That sounds like excellent teamwork," said Rebecca, smiling. "I hope you enjoy choosing a bunny, Ella. I should get back to work now — the horses need feeding." With a quick wave, she headed out of the barn.

"Bye, Rebecca!" called the princesses.

"Can I choose a rabbit right now?" asked Ella.

"Of course you can! I'll show you where they are." Rosalind skipped down the length of the barn, avoiding a bucket of water that stood by the sheep pen.

Summer and Lottie ran after her and they stopped next to a large hutch that was full of hay.

"Come and look, Ella," said Summer. "You're going to love these bunnies. They're so cute!"

CHAPTER FOUR

Daisy the Baby Rabbit

Ella hurried to join the others and crouched down in front of the hutch. There was no movement inside. A bundle of small, fluffy shapes lay huddled together in a dark corner. "They're sleeping!" she whispered.

"They were born a few weeks ago, just before the start of the school year," Rosalind told her. "There are five of them altogether."

Summer undid the latch on the door. "There you go! You can pet them if you want."

"Aw! They're lovely." Ella reached in and gently touched the rabbits. Their fur was warm and soft. There were two brown rabbits, two gray ones, and a honey-colored one with a little pink nose.

"Which bunny would you like?" asked Lottie. "None of them even have names yet."

The rabbits opened their eyes at the sound of the girls' voices. The gray ones pricked up their ears. The honey-colored rabbit hopped along the run. Then she looked up at Ella and twitched her pink nose.

"I'd like this one." Ella pointed to her. "And I'd like to call her . . ." She thought for a moment. "I'd like to call her Daisy."

"That's a pretty name!" Rosalind carefully lifted the honey-colored rabbit out of the hutch and gave her to Ella.

"Hello, Daisy. You're so cute!" Ella stroked the bunny's floppy ears. They felt like velvet. Daisy's nose twitched and she wriggled a little. Ella smiled and pressed her cheek against the bunny's soft fur.

"She likes you!" said Lottie, grinning.

"I like her, too," said Ella. "I'm glad I'm not going to be the only one here without a pet."

Just then there were heavy footsteps outside the barn and a girl with thin, dark hair came in. Ella recognized her. It was Molly, the girl who'd complained about Summer's parrot.

"Didn't you hear the bell for dinner?" snapped the older girl. "It rang ten minutes ago. Miss Goldwin made me come and find you."

"No, we didn't hear it," said Lottie. "Thanks for telling us, Molly."

Molly ignored Lottie's thanks. She folded her arms and glared at them. "Who said you could take one of the rabbits out of their hutch? No one's allowed to touch them yet."

"Miss Goldwin said we could," said Rosalind. "This one belongs to Ella now."

Molly snorted. "Poor rabbit! I bet you don't know anything about looking after it. You're not even holding it right."

"Oh! Well, I've never had a rabbit before, but I will look after her really carefully." Ella bit her lip. She didn't want the older girl to be angry with her. She just wanted to make friends. "Would you like to hold her? You can show me how to do it."

She walked toward Molly, but as she got closer, Daisy wriggled frantically. Ella clutched the little rabbit, afraid she was going to leap out of her arms. Her foot caught on a bale of hay and she tripped, bumping into the older girl.

"Careful!" Molly stepped backward, knocking over the bucket of water by the sheep stall.

Water gushed everywhere. The metal bucket rolled across the ground with a hollow clang. Molly slipped, her arms flapping. Then she landed on her bottom on the wet floor.

"Are you okay?" Ella wanted to help the older girl, but Daisy was still wriggling.

"Here you go! Take my hand." Lottie held out her arm, but Molly wouldn't take it.

The older girl leapt to her feet, her face bright red. Her skirt and sweater were

soaked, and bits of hay and dirt were stuck to her clothes. "Ugh! I'm wet and muddy, and it's all your fault!"

"I'm really sorry!" Ella felt her cheeks flush. "I didn't mean to bump into you."

"You *will* be sorry!" hissed Molly. "I'm going to make you all wish you'd never come to this Academy. I'm a captain and I can stop you from coming down to the pet barn if I want to!" She gave them a final glare and walked off.

Rosalind's eyes were fierce. "I don't know why she has to be like that! I'm going to tell Miss Goldwin what she said."

"Don't!" said Lottie. "It'll just make things worse."

"Are you all right, Ella?" asked Summer. "Don't worry, it was just an accident."

"I know," said Ella. "I just wish I hadn't been so clumsy." She gave Daisy one more stroke and put her back with the other little bunnies. "I'll come back and see you really soon," she told the baby rabbit.

She hoped the older girl, Molly, didn't really plan to stop them from coming to the pet barn. She wanted to spend time with her new baby rabbit more than anything!

CHAPTER FIVE

Sharing a Secret

Over the next few days, Ella settled in to life at Harebell Castle. She got used to sharing a bunk bed with Summer in their room in Seahorse Tower, and she even liked the school dinners, which always ended with a large serving of dessert!

With the help of Rebecca, who looked after the pet barn, she had learned all about taking care of baby rabbits. She knew what food Daisy needed and how often to clean her cage out. The princesses were supposed to check on their pets every morning and night. It wasn't easy, as school life was very busy and Molly, the dark-haired captain, seemed to think of lots of jobs for Ella and her friends to do.

Ella liked her new teachers, too. The only one who made her nervous was Lady Eggley, the Royal Skills teacher, who had perfectly smooth hair and eyes as sharp as needles. At first, Ella had liked going into the magnificent Throne Room for her lessons. The shelves were full of silver trophies, and the golden throne gleamed as if it was polished every day. But Lady Eggley swooped down on Ella every time she made a little mistake, telling Ella that her curtsies were terrible and her tiara was always crooked.

Ella began to dread the Royal Skills lessons and talked to the others about it back in Seahorse Tower.

"Don't worry about it," said Lottie. "Lady Eggley is a royal fusspot."

"I've heard that she's crazy about eating carrots and always keeps some in her bedroom," said Rosalind. "Maybe her name should be Lady Carroty instead of Lady Eggley."

Ella giggled, feeling a little better.

Summer put down her book and climbed off the top bunk. "Now that we're all together, why don't we go down to the pet barn and see the animals? You can check on your rabbit, Ella, and we can look at the other baby bunnies, too."

The door suddenly swung open and Molly stood there, smirking. "Oh good! You're all here. I need you to help with some chores."

"But we were just going down to check on our pets," protested Ella. "We don't want Rebecca to think we're not looking after them."

"No, Rebecca wouldn't be pleased if you didn't take care of your rabbit," said Molly, with a spiteful look in her eye. "But first, all the rooms in the tower need dusting and the corridor needs sweeping. Hurry up now!" And she slammed the door.

"Every time we try to go to the pet barn, she invents a job for us," said Lottie. "I haven't seen Strawberry for three days. If this keeps up, Rebecca will have to report us to Miss Goldwin for not looking after our animals. We might not even be allowed to keep our pets anymore. We *have* to get away from Molly!"

"I wish her room wasn't right at the start of the corridor," said Summer. "No one can leave the tower without her seeing them."

Rosalind folded her arms. "We can beat her easily. All we need are some ninja moves."

"Some what?" said Ella, surprised.

Rosalind put her hand over her mouth. "Oops!"

Lottie rolled her eyes. "Rosalind! I think we should tell you our secret anyway, Ella. You're one of us now."

Ella turned pink. "Thanks, Lottie!"

"Let's explain later. We don't want Molly to hear us," said Summer.

After dinner, they found an empty classroom downstairs instead of returning to Seahorse Tower. Rosalind took out her flashlight. "Don't turn the lights on. We don't want anyone to know we're in here."

Ella felt a swooping feeling in her stomach. Now she would find out what the secret was!

"First of all, you have to promise not to tell anyone about this," said Lottie.

Ella nodded quickly. "I won't tell."

Rosalind took a deep breath. "You see, we're the Rescue Princesses and we rescue animals in danger."

"I was the first one to set up the club," said Lottie. "Well, it was my sister, Emily, actually. She rescued some deer in Mistberg Forest with the help of her friends. But when she left home to go to boarding school, I took over."

"That's when I joined," added Rosalind. "It was me, Lottie, Amina, and Isabella. You haven't met Amina or Isabella yet because they're not coming here till next semester."

"Then I met everyone in the springtime," said Summer. "We rescued a snow leopard with the help of a princess named Maya."

"So you'll be the twelfth Rescue Princess," said Lottie. "But the number isn't really important. The point is we help animals, no matter how dangerous it is, and we have magic jewels that help us, *and* we know ninja moves, too! We even have a book about ninja moves hidden upstairs."

"Wow!" Ella stared at them all. "That is so cool."

"Would you like to join?" asked Lottie.

"Yes, please!" Ella beamed. "It sounds very exciting."

"Good! Tomorrow we'll use our ninja moves to get past Molly," said Lottie, pushing back her red curls. "We'll wait till classes are over and then sneak out before she can stop us."

"Oh, one more thing!" said Rosalind. "I made a few more rings during the vacation just in case we needed them, and yours is a yellow diamond." She dropped a ring with a beautiful yellow jewel into Ella's hand. "Pressing the jewel lets us talk to one another."

"Thank you!" Ella slid the ring onto her finger and pressed the diamond. The jewel lit up instantly and the rings on her friends' hands shone brightly, too. Lottie had a ruby ring, Rosalind had a deep-blue sapphire, and Summer's jewel was a beautiful purple amethyst.

The princesses were still admiring their magical rings when the door creaked open. Ella swung around and was dazzled when someone turned on the light.

"Hey! What's going on?" asked a voice.

The girls leapt up. Lottie and Summer stuffed their hands behind their backs to hide their glowing rings. Ella tripped over a chair and grabbed onto a table to keep herself from falling over.

"You should have knocked," snapped Rosalind. "You made us jump."

Ella got her balance back and looked up, worried that Molly had found them.

There were five girls standing in the doorway, and thankfully none of them was Molly. The girl at the front had long red curls and looked familiar somehow.

"Emily!" said Lottie.

The girl with the red curls grinned. "Hi, little sis! Sorry we made you jump. We heard voices and wondered what was going on. What were you doing in the dark?"

"We're inviting a new girl into the Rescue Princesses," said Lottie. "It's okay!" she told the others. "These are the old members of the group. This is Lulu, Clarabel, Jaminta, Freya, and my sister Emily. They all live in Coral Tower."

The older princesses smiled. "We heard

you'd kept the Rescue Princesses going and had lots of adventures," said a girl with black hair and lionlike eyes. "Well done!"

"Thanks, Lulu," said Lottie. "Actually, we're organizing a mission right now." She told the older girls about the problem with Molly and what had happened in the pet barn.

"Molly's being so unfair," added Rosalind. "So we're going to use our ninja moves to get out of Seahorse Tower and away from her! Otherwise we can't look after our pets."

Emily looked a little worried. "Well, be careful when you're sneaking around. I've heard that this castle has hidden doors and secret passages!"

"That's right." Lulu nodded. "After all, this place was a real castle in the olden days, before it became a school!"

"I wish we could find some of the secret places," said Lottie. "Then we could hide from Molly and her endless list of chores!"

"Be careful, little sis," Emily said to Lottie. "You have a way of getting into trouble."

"Oh, don't worry!" said Lottie. "We're not babies. We know exactly what to do!"

CHAPTER SIX

The Ninja
Bumblebee

The next day crept by slowly. At last,
classes ended and the four girls hurried
back to Seahorse Tower.

Once the bedroom door was closed,
Rosalind lifted up her mattress and
took out a book hidden underneath.
It had a black cover with *The Book of
Ninja* written on it in gold letters. Ella
noticed how old it looked. Some of the
pages were worn and speckled with
brown marks.

"I had a quick look last night, and I think I've found the perfect thing," said Rosalind, flicking through the pages. "This move will distract Molly while we sneak out." She turned the book around to show them.

The picture depicted someone dangling a shoe out of a window using a piece of string. Another picture showed the person in the room below looking out of the window at the floating shoe in amazement.

"We can surprise Molly and make her stare out of the window while we escape," said Summer. "There's a bathroom above her bedroom, so we should be able to get in there easily."

"But what should we put on the end of the string?" asked Lottie. "If we're not careful she'll realize that it's a trick right away."

"We could dangle one of our teddy bears," suggested Summer.

"I'm not dangling mine." Lottie tucked her teddy bear under her arm. "He might fall off!"

"It should be something that's supposed to fly," said Ella. "Then she'll think it's real. Something like a butterfly or a — I know!" She jumped to her feet, opened a drawer, and pulled out a pair of striped black-and-yellow socks. "A bumblebee!"

"Ella! That's a great idea!" said Rosalind. "Those stripes *do* look like a bee. We can stuff the sock with paper and put wings on it. Then when Molly looks out of the window, she'll wonder if she's seeing a giant bee."

There were heavy footsteps and the door opened. Ella quickly hid the striped socks behind her back.

Molly looked in and scowled. "There'll

be a room inspection in ten minutes, so don't think you can run off anywhere."

"Molly, I just want to visit my rabbit today," began Ella. "Do you think —"

"Forget it!" snapped Molly. "You don't have time!" And she closed the door with a bang.

Lottie waited a moment and then opened the door a crack to check that the older girl was gone. "That's it! She's had her chance. Let's put together our ninja trick."

Together, they stuffed one of the socks with paper to give the bee a round body. Then Summer found two pieces of clear plastic that they cut into wing shapes and stuck on with tape.

Ella got her sewing kit and took out a spool of blue cotton. "If we use blue-colored thread, then hopefully she won't spot it. The cotton will be camouflaged against the sky."

"Be as quick as you can," urged Rosalind. "Molly will be back any minute."

Finally, the fake bumblebee was ready.

"I'll take the bee up to the bathroom and dangle it from the window," said Rosalind. "You three go ahead and sneak out. I'll catch up with you in the pet barn." Stuffing the bee under her sweater, Rosalind ran swiftly upstairs.

"Okay, is everyone ready?" whispered Lottie. "Let's get closer."

Ella, Lottie, and Summer tiptoed down the corridor. They heard heavy footsteps inside Molly's room. Lottie signaled for them to stop, but the older girl didn't come out. They crept even closer and peeked around the door.

Molly was standing in front of the mirror doing different poses. She put her hands on her hips. Then she folded her arms and grinned at the mirror. Ella had the urge to giggle and slapped her hand over her mouth.

There was a soft tapping sound. A yellow-and-black striped bee-sock swung through the air and thudded gently against the window.

Ella had a sudden brainstorm. "I know what will help," she murmured to Summer.

Whump! The bee-sock bumped against the window again. Molly caught sight of it and turned around.

"Bzzzzz!" Ella began making a soft buzzing sound. "Bzz, bzz!"

Molly stepped closer to the window. "Huh! What's going on?"

"Bzz!" Ella got a bit louder, and Summer and Lottie joined in.

The bee-sock outside the window began bobbing up and down in the air,

as if it was doing a little bumblebee dance.

Molly ran to the window, opened it, and stuck her head out. The bee-sock soared over her head into the sky. "No way! That bee was enormous!"

With one final buzz, Ella, Lottie, and Summer raced past the doorway and down the corridor. They ran until they reached the bottom of the stairs, then they collapsed into giggles.

"She thought it was real!" gasped Summer.

"I bet she'll tell everyone she saw the biggest bee in the world!" snorted Lottie.

"It was a shame the bee had to buzz off in the end!" giggled Ella.

Still laughing, they made their way out of school and across the lawn to the pet barn. Lottie ran off to the stables to see her pony, Strawberry, while Ella and

Summer went to visit the rabbits. The barn was dark and cozy. Animals rustled in the hay and now and then the lambs bleated.

"Rebecca's not here," said Summer, looking around. "Maybe she's busy in the fields."

"I hope Daisy still remembers me," said Ella.

"Of course she will," replied Summer. "It's only been a few days. She wouldn't forget you that quickly."

They crouched down next to the rabbit run. The two gray rabbits were asleep in a corner and the brown ones were nibbling on some hay. Daisy was standing by the side of the pen, her little pink nose tilted upward as if she'd been waiting for them.

"Hello, Daisy." Ella leaned over and stroked her honey-colored fur.

Daisy twitched her nose at Ella's hand

and hopped up and down the run in excitement. Ella laughed. Then as soon as the little bunny stopped jumping, she lifted her out of the run for a cuddle.

"Aw, she's so cute!" Summer rubbed Daisy's ears. "I'm just going to see the hens. I want to know if any chicks have hatched today."

Ella smiled. "Call me if you see any." She sat down on a hay bale and rested Daisy in her lap. "Next time I come I'm going to bring you a treat," she told the little rabbit. "Would you like some carrots? I wish you could live in my bedroom with me. That would be so awesome."

Suddenly Daisy pricked up her ears. Then she stood up on her hind legs, sniffing the air.

"What is it?" said Ella. "Can you smell something strange?"

Daisy crawled and hid her nose under Ella's arm.

Puzzled, Ella got up, holding her rabbit tight. She crossed to the barn window and looked out.

Molly was striding across the lawn with a huge frown on her face.

"Oh no!" whispered Ella. "She must have figured out that we snuck away. We have to hide!"

CHAPTER SEVEN

The Wonders of the Throne Room

Ella hurried through the barn, calling to Summer as loudly as she dared. Summer poked her head out of the henhouse.

"Molly's coming," hissed Ella. "We've got to do something!"

"I'll go this way." Summer pointed to the back door. "I'll find Lottie and we'll meet you back at Seahorse Tower."

Ella nodded. Through the window, she could see Molly getting closer. She dashed out of the main door and ran

along the side of the barn until she came
to a wooden bench. She crouched down
behind it, hoping that Molly hadn't
spotted her running from the barn.

Daisy wriggled in her arms. Ella stroked
the rabbit's soft ears. In her panic about
Molly, she'd almost forgotten that she
was holding the little bunny.

Molly marched straight inside without
looking in the direction of the bench. Ella
got up from her hiding place and tiptoed
back to the barn door. Molly was leaning
over the rabbit hutch, counting the number
of baby rabbits. Then she sat down on a
hay bale and folded her arms.

She's waiting until I come back, thought
Ella.

Nervously, she pushed a black curl
behind her ear and wondered what to
do. She had to talk to the others. They
would have some ideas for a ninja move.

With one last look at the barn, she rushed across the lawn, darting behind the topiary statues and hoping she wouldn't be seen.

Luckily, the castle entrance was empty. Ella hurried toward the stairs, stopping when she heard Lady Eggley's voice drifting down from the balcony. "There's such a terrible draft in this castle! Why must the princesses always leave the front door wide open? I shall close it myself!"

Ella's eyes widened. If a teacher caught her bringing a rabbit into the castle, she'd be in big trouble. And Lady Eggley was the very last teacher she wanted to be caught by! Looking left and right, Ella darted through the nearest open door and into the Throne Room.

She heard Lady Eggley's high-heeled shoes tapping on the stone floor outside.

Where could she hide? The room was nearly bare, with just a strip of red carpet leading to the magnificent golden throne. Pictures of kings and queens hung on the walls, and the shelves had rows of silver trophies.

Ella spotted a small door in the corner of the room. She thought it must be a storage closet. She ran to it and pulled the handle. It was locked. Quickly, she ducked down behind the golden throne before she was seen. Her heart thumped and she hugged Daisy tightly.

"Lady Eggley, I have some bad news." Molly's voice rang out clearly.

Ella peeked around the throne and looked through the open doorway. She saw Molly standing next to the teacher in the hallway outside. She watched the older girl curtsy perfectly. Ella stifled a sigh. Why couldn't she curtsy like that?

"What is it, Molly?" asked Lady Eggley. "Nothing serious, I hope."

"I've just seen a new girl bring a rabbit into the castle," said Molly in a shocked voice. "Her name is Ella. I'm afraid that as a captain in her tower, I find her very badly behaved."

Lady Eggley's eyebrows rose and she tutted.

"And her fingernails are really dirty," added Molly.

Ella looked at her fingernails. She had to admit, they were pretty grubby.

"Well, there is no excuse for that!" declared Lady Eggley. "Find her and bring her straight to me. I will wait here."

Ella peered around the edge of the golden throne again. She could still see Lady Eggley standing in the hallway outside. The teacher frowned and smoothed her perfect hair.

Ella shifted uncomfortably. Her legs were aching and Daisy was wriggling, but she knew if she stood up she'd be seen. She hoped that Lady Eggley would get tired of waiting in one place and walk away, giving her the chance to escape.

Summer and Lottie came running through the front door into the hallway.

"Princesses! You must not run inside the Academy," said Lady Eggley.

"Sorry!" Summer curtsied.

"Have either of you seen a princess named Ella and a runaway rabbit?" demanded Lady Eggley.

"No, sorry!" said Lottie. "We don't know where she is."

"Well, if you see her, please send her to me. I will not permit animals or princesses to run wild!" said the teacher. Then she muttered to herself, "This is what comes of turning Harebell Castle into a pet club."

Ella heard Lottie and Summer walk away, but Lady Eggley remained in the hallway, tapping one high-heeled shoe. Ella looked down at Daisy and saw that she'd fallen asleep.

To try and take her mind off her aching legs, Ella gazed at the ornate carvings on the golden throne. Being so close, she could see every shape and swirl. Little red rubies sparkled along the throne's arms, and green emeralds glistened on the top. A red velvet cloth wrapped around the lower part of the throne and reached down to the floor.

Ella gazed at the small shells carved into the back of the throne. They were so beautiful! One shell gleamed more brightly than the others, and she traced her finger across its fanlike shape.

Then, suddenly, the shell moved.

Ella paused; surely she must have imagined it! Slowly, she touched the golden shell again and pushed it.

The shell moved smoothly to the side. There was a muffled clunk from the corner, and the door of the closet swung slightly open.

Ella turned and stared. Golden light poured through the crack in the door. It couldn't be a closet . . . but then, what was it? And how had this golden shell unlocked it?

A tingle ran down her back.

"What's that noise?" asked Lady Eggley.

Ella peered over the top of the throne. The teacher was looking all around the hall. She must have heard the clunking noise as the door opened! What if she came into the Throne Room? Ella's heart thumped and she pushed the shell again.

She had to close the door quickly. But the door wouldn't move.

Ella tried again. She put Daisy down on the floor so that she could use both hands. The little rabbit woke up and twitched her nose. Ella pushed the shell with all her strength.

This time it moved a little. The door swung back until it was almost shut and only a tiny glint of light could be seen. Ella was just about to reach across and close the door completely when Lady Eggley marched into the room.

"Who's there?" said the teacher. "I demand that you come out at once."

Ella's heart sank. Quickly, she hid Daisy underneath the red cloth that circled the bottom of the throne. Then she took a deep breath and stood up. "Hello, Lady Eggley." She gave a wobbly curtsy. "It's me, Princess Ella."

CHAPTER EIGHT

Ella in Trouble

Lady Eggley looked Ella up and down,
a deep frown creasing her forehead.

Ella suddenly realized how dusty
her skirt looked, and that bits of hay
were sticking to her sweater. "Um, I can
explain —" she began.

"You can *explain*?" said Lady Eggley.
"Nothing you say can excuse such unruly
behavior! This is *not* what we expect of
our princesses."

Ella's cheeks flushed. "I'm really sorry."

"Hiding like that — how sneaky! And just look at the state of you!" Lady Eggley took hold of Ella's hand and examined her fingernails.

Just then, Molly ran into the room. "Oh, Lady Eggley. You found her." She cast a mean grin at Ella behind the teacher's back. "But where's the rabbit?"

Ella hoped that Daisy was still hidden under the red cloth beneath the throne.

Lady Eggley's attention was fixed on Ella's fingernails. "You must learn to scrub these nails thoroughly. Do it at least ten times a day!" She let go of Ella's hand. "Now, unless you have some good reason for being in here, I will have to find you a punishment."

Molly's grin widened.

"Did someone say punishment?" Rebecca walked in. Her eyes flicked from Ella's worried face to Molly's grin.

"I'm afraid that Ella has been very naughty." Lady Eggley brushed a speck of dust from her sleeve. "She came in here by herself without permission. She hid from me, and she is *not* clean and tidy. Therefore I shall be deciding on a suitable punishment for her."

"Excellent!" said Rebecca firmly. "I need someone to help me carry lots of bags of hay. That can be Ella's punishment. I'm sure you won't object, Lady Eggley; I really need the extra help."

"Of course!" said the teacher graciously. "I will leave her in your charge. And remember, Princess Ella, I shall be checking your fingernails from now on." She nodded to Rebecca and swept out of the room.

Molly glanced around the room again, and Ella knew she was still looking for Daisy.

"Run along then, Molly," said Rebecca.

Molly looked annoyed but had no choice but to go.

Rebecca turned to Ella and smiled. "Are you all right, Ella? I saw your friends outside the pet barn just now and they told me about how difficult Molly has been. I'd started to think you didn't want to look after your little rabbit, but I hear that isn't true."

"It isn't true at all!" cried Ella. "I really *do* want to take care of Daisy. It was awful when Molly wouldn't give us time to come down to the barn." Her eyes flicked sideways, expecting to catch a glimpse of the rabbit. Where *was* Daisy?

"Well, Lady Eggley is expecting you to help me, so we'd better head to the barn," said Rebecca. "Moving the hay is actually quite a fun job, I think! And you'll be able to say hello to your bunny again."

Ella flushed. She knew she should explain to Rebecca that her rabbit was here in the Throne Room, but what if the pet keeper was really shocked? What if she was so angry that she wouldn't let her keep Daisy any more?

Ella decided she should be honest. "Um, the thing is," she began. "I left the pet barn in a hurry, and—"

"Oh, don't worry!" said Rebecca. "If you'd rather help carry the hay tomorrow, then that's fine. It doesn't have to be done today. I won't tell Lady Eggley if you don't!" She gave Ella a wink.

Ella swallowed. Rebecca hadn't really understood.

Just then, Lottie, Summer, and Rosalind ran in. "There you are!" said Rosalind. "We were beginning to think you'd vanished."

"Hello, girls! Well, I must get going." Rebecca marched to the door. "There are ponies to feed and groom, hamster cages to clean out, and goodness knows what else!" She was gone before Ella could say anything more.

"What happened, Ella?" asked Lottie. "We couldn't find you anywhere."

"I was here all the time, but I had to hide when Lady Eggley stood outside in the hallway." Ella dived behind the throne to look for her rabbit.

"Are you okay?" asked Rosalind, watching her in surprise.

"I have to find Daisy. She's somewhere around here." Ella pulled up the red material that circled the bottom of the throne and felt around underneath. Her fingers swept across empty floorboards. She crouched right down behind the throne and put her head under the red cloth.

There was nothing there.

"Daisy! Where are you?" Ella looked around frantically. "I put her here. She couldn't have just disappeared!"

The other girls peered underneath the red cloth, too.

"She can't be very far away. There's nowhere else to hide," said Summer.

The girls spread out, checking behind chairs and even on the trophy shelves.

Ella suddenly remembered the golden shell and the mysterious door. "Oh, I almost forgot!" She ran to the corner. "I thought this was a locked closet, but when I pushed one shell on the back of the throne the door opened like magic. I tried to close it, but . . ." She caught her breath. The door was only open a tiny crack, but it was still large enough for a baby rabbit to squeeze through.

"You mean the door opens with a magic switch?" said Lottie. "I'd like to see that!"

Ella pulled the door open, and golden light poured through. Inside was an alcove with an old-fashioned lantern. The light from the lantern shone onto a stone passage that curved away around a corner.

"Wow!" Rosalind gasped, peering into the passageway.

"I wonder where it leads," said Summer.

"Poor Daisy!" said Ella. "She must have squeezed through when no one was looking. We have to find her."

Bong! The castle bell rang out three times and then footsteps came down the hallway. Ella closed the mysterious door quickly and stood in front of it.

Molly came in. "That was the bell for dinner," she told them. "Hurry up — or I'll tell Lady Eggley that you were messing around in here again."

Rosalind squeezed Ella's hand and

whispered. "Don't worry! We'll come back."

Ella followed the others out of the room. She knew Molly was watching her and she tried hard not to look back at the door. *I'll explore that secret passage once Molly's not looking!* she promised herself. *She won't stop me from finding Daisy.*

CHAPTER NINE

The Hidden Passageway

Dinner was a delicious cheese pizza with salad, but Ella didn't taste any of it. She gulped down her food while the others whispered about getting flashlights from upstairs.

"That lantern inside the door might not light up the whole passageway," said Rosalind. "We need to take flashlights, just in case."

Ella could see Molly sitting at a table

nearby and caught the older girl looking at her a few times.

When they'd finished, Summer went back for the flashlights. The other girls hung around the entrance hall, waiting for a chance to slip into the Throne Room without anyone seeing them.

Ella linked her fingers together, trying to stop her hands from shaking. She couldn't bear the thought of Daisy all alone in the stone passageway. She hoped they would find her quickly.

Summer returned with the flashlights, but it took a long time for all the other girls to finally leave the dining hall and go upstairs to their towers. At last, the hallway emptied. The princesses slipped into the Throne Room without switching on the light and closed the door behind them.

Ella went behind the throne and fumbled for the golden shell. "Here it is!"

She pushed the shell and it slid sideways. There was a muffled clunk and the door in the corner swung open. Light poured into the room from the old-fashioned lantern on the alcove inside.

"Quickly!" hissed Rosalind. "Let's go before someone comes in and finds us!"

The girls bundled into the stone passage and Lottie closed the door behind them.

"Wait, Lottie!" said Summer. "What if there isn't a way to open the door from this side?"

"There must be!" said Lottie.

The girls looked at the door, but there was no handle on the inside and no lever on the wall either.

"Uh . . . sorry!" said Lottie. "I didn't mean to shut us in. But there'll be a way out at the other end, right?"

The others looked at one another worriedly.

Then Ella said, "There must be another way out. Let's just find Daisy."

Rosalind led the way along the stone corridor. After the first bend, light from the lantern faded and the girls turned on their flashlights. Ella shone hers at the floor, hoping to see Daisy leaping along the passage in front of them. She longed to find the little bunny and stroke her warm fur.

The passageway twisted again and again. The princesses followed it left and right, and their feet began to ache.

"I didn't think we'd have to walk so far," said Lottie. "It seems like we've been in here for a long time."

"Ooh, look at the ceiling," said Summer, shining her flashlight up. "There are golden shells up there that look just like the one on the back of the throne."

The other girls looked up. "You're

right," said Ella. "They have the same fan shape as the one that opened the mystery door. I hope that means we're going the right way."

They came to some steps and followed them down. At the bottom Rosalind stopped suddenly, making the others bump into her.

"Rosy! Don't stop like that!" cried Lottie.

"Shh!" said Rosalind. "I can hear something."

A low clanking noise came from above them, mixed with the sound of muffled voices.

"It sounds a bit like people washing dishes," said Ella at last. "Do you think we're below the kitchen?"

"Yes, we must be!" said Rosalind, her blue eyes gleaming. "And maybe that's why Daisy came down here. Maybe she smelled vegetables and she felt hungry!"

"Let's keep going," said Lottie.

They hurried along the narrow corridor. The stone floor became uneven and Ella noticed that the walls were damp. The passageway opened out into a small, empty room.

"Look!" Ella shone her flashlight at the door. "There's a way out, and it has that golden shell on it again."

"Hold on!" Rosalind frowned. "Where's Daisy? She couldn't have turned the handle and opened that door."

"Look, there's a hole." Lottie shone her flashlight at a small gap at the bottom of the wall where a brick was missing. "I bet Daisy got out that way. It's just the right size for a rabbit!"

Ella crouched down close to the hole and caught the smell of cooking. "You're right — she could easily have gone through there."

Lottie pulled at the door but it didn't open. "It's stuck! Now what are we going to do?"

Rosalind tried the door, too. "I hope it's not locked."

"Let's try pulling it at the same time," suggested Ella, and she and Rosalind both grabbed the door handle.

"One, two, three, go!" said Rosalind, and they pulled together.

The door flew open, sending both girls flying backward.

"Are you all right?" Summer asked, helping them up.

"I'm fine." Ella rubbed her elbow. "I just hope no one heard the noise."

"It's all right — there's no one here," said Lottie, who had gone through to look around. "It looks like this is some kind of storage room."

The other princesses followed her into

the room, closing the door carefully behind them. The room was very small and had no windows. Tall cupboards lined the walls and baskets of fruit and vegetables were stacked on one side. Stone steps led up to a half-open door, and beyond that was the sound of people talking and banging saucepans.

"We must be right next to the kitchen," muttered Rosalind.

"There's no sign of Daisy, though." Summer shone her flashlight into the corners of the room.

"Poor Daisy!" said Ella. "I wish Molly hadn't stopped us from looking earlier. We might have found her right away." She ran up the steps to the half-open door, stopping when she heard a familiar voice.

"Where is my plate? I don't want to wait forever, you know," said Lady Eggley snootily. "I've had a very busy day and I want to go to bed soon. Please hurry up and put my snacks on the cart."

Ella's heart sank. Where was Daisy? If Lady Eggley saw her, they would all be in big trouble!

CHAPTER TEN

The Bunny Hunt

Ella signaled to the others to be quiet. Then she peeked around the door. She could see Lady Eggley and one of the cooks, who was wearing a large green apron. Next to Lady Eggley was a small catering cart with wheels. Ella tried to see if there was anything on the cart but the teacher was blocking her view.

"Oh good. You've done it *at last*," said Lady Eggley. "I'll take this to my room now. Good night." Then she left the

kitchen, pushing the cart in front of her. The *click-clack* of her footsteps grew fainter.

"Lady Eggley's gone," Ella whispered to the others.

"That lady has no manners," muttered the cook, banging a saucepan down on the table. "No manners at all! Now, what's all this? Who's made a mess of my lettuces?"

Rosalind nudged Ella. "Something knocked over the box of lettuce — look!"

Ella saw the cook pick up the fallen lettuces and put them back in the box. "I bet that was Daisy!" she whispered. "Maybe she's hiding somewhere."

At last, the cook finished cleaning up. She hung up her apron and switched off the light. As soon as she left, the princesses turned their flashlights back on and dashed into the kitchen.

They searched under tables and inside cupboards. They peered into the fridge and even took the lids off the saucepans to check inside.

"I can't think of anywhere else to look," said Rosalind.

"Where *are* you, Daisy?" Ella said softly.

"I don't think she's here," said Summer at last. "Maybe she knocked over that box of lettuce and then hopped away."

"She might have gone this way." Lottie hurried down the passageway and the others followed.

Ella felt an uneasy wriggling deep down in her tummy. She didn't know her way around the school very well and it was even more confusing in the dark. How had Daisy managed to hop so far without getting tired? She was only a baby rabbit, after all!

"Here's the art room and next door is the library," said Lottie. "Rosalind and Ella, you look in the library, and Summer and I will search in here."

Ella followed Rosalind into the library. The two girls went along every single shelf of books and checked carefully under the chairs and tables.

"This is really strange," said Ella, pushing back her dark, wavy hair.

"What do you mean?" asked Rosalind.

"I don't understand how Daisy went so far." Ella bit her lip. "It's as if she just disappeared."

"It *is* a little weird," agreed Rosalind. "But she must be somewhere."

Lottie opened the library door. "There are no bunnies in the art room. Any luck in here?"

Ella and Rosalind shook their heads.

The princesses kept on searching. They checked three classrooms and then tiptoed into a new corridor with thick red carpets.

"Watch out, everyone," hissed Lottie. "This is where the teachers sleep."

"We should go back," said Summer. "We could get in so much trouble."

"Maybe we can take a peek inside their bedrooms." Lottie tiptoed up to the nearest door and pulled down the handle. "I'll only open the door a tiny bit."

"Lottie!" gasped Ella. "What if the teacher wakes up and sees you looking in?"

There was a low snort from inside the room, followed by a voice saying. "Hmm? What's that? Your dirty fingernails are a disgrace!" Then there was a creaking sound followed by silence.

Lottie opened the door very slightly and there was another loud snort from the bed. "I think that's Lady Eggley," she whispered with a giggle.

"Not so loud," muttered Rosalind.

Ella didn't dare to shine her flashlight into the room. She peered through the darkness. "It does look like Lady Eggley," she whispered to the others. "And look, there's the snack cart that she wheeled out of the kitchen."

The cart was covered by a long piece of cloth that gaped open at one end, revealing another shelf underneath. Ella looked closer. Was that a small furry shape next to the cart? "Daisy!" she whispered joyfully.

The furry shape twitched and two ears pricked up.

"Oh, Daisy! What are you doing in there?" murmured Summer.

"I bet she rode all the way here on the bottom of that cart, and Lady Eggley didn't even know," said Lottie, giggling. "She had no idea that she was giving a rabbit a ride!"

Rosalind nudged her. "Shh, Lottie! You're still too loud —" She broke off as the teacher turned over in bed.

Then a muffled voice said, "Wretched girls! I can hear them talking. They should *not* be running around in the middle of the night!"

Ella gasped and waved her hand at Lottie. "Close the door!" she mouthed. "Quickly, before she sees us!"

CHAPTER ELEVEN

Lady Eggley's Bedroom

Lottie shut the teacher's door. The girls stood still, holding their breath and listening for sounds from inside.

"I can't hear any creaking so I don't think she got out of bed," whispered Summer. "Maybe she was just talking in her sleep."

"We need to get Daisy out of there," said Lottie. "If Lady Eggley catches the rabbit in her room, she'll go crazy!"

"Can you get Daisy to come to you,

Ella?" asked Summer. "She loves you. Maybe if she sees you she'll come over."

"I'll try." Ella's heart thumped as she slowly pulled down the door handle.

Loud snores filled the bedroom and Ella felt relieved. Lady Eggley must be asleep. She saw Lottie put her fingers over her mouth to stop a giggle.

Kneeling down, Ella held out her hand and whispered as quietly as she could, "Daisy! Come over here." But the rabbit twitched her nose naughtily and bounced away behind the cart.

Ella straightened up. "I'm going in to get her," she whispered to the others. "Rosalind, could you hold the door for me?"

Rosalind held the door open, wincing when it creaked a little. Ella crept over to the cart, but Daisy wasn't hiding there.

She wasn't on the bottom shelf or behind the dangling cloth.

Ella bit her lip. The longer it took to find the little rabbit, the more likely they all were to get caught. She tiptoed around the room, looking for Daisy on the floor. Then she knelt down and checked under the bed. She looked into all the corners and behind the wastebasket. She couldn't see Daisy anywhere.

Lady Eggley was still snoring. Now and then, she muttered something in her sleep.

Lottie came in and started looking, too. Ella peered behind the perfume bottles and hand mirrors on the teacher's dresser. She turned around, wondering where else to look. Something moved on the bed and Ella froze. On top of the sleeping teacher sat a little floppy-eared bunny!

"Can you see her?" hissed Lottie.

Ella put a finger to her lips and then pointed at Daisy, who was hopping along the blanket that covered Lady Eggley.

"She must have jumped up there," whispered Lottie.

Ella wondered how she was going to pick up Daisy without waking the teacher. Lady Eggley grunted in her sleep and then smacked her lips together. Ella held her breath, but the teacher didn't open her eyes.

Daisy hopped over Lady Eggley's stomach until she reached her neck. Then, to Ella's horror, she nibbled at the teacher's chin.

"What's that?" muttered Lady Eggley. "Tickling is not allowed in class!"

Ella ducked down and crawled across the floor to the bed. She had to get to Daisy before the bunny did something

even naughtier! She peered at the sleeping teacher just as the rabbit jumped onto the pillow and began sniffing at Lady Eggley's ear.

Ella tried to take hold of Daisy. Her hand brushed against her soft fur, but the bunny slipped under her fingers and sprang off the pillow onto the bedside table. Lady Eggley rolled over in bed. Ella waited until the teacher had stopped moving, then she crawled after Daisy.

A plate of carrot sticks lay on the bedside table. Next to it was a yellow book with the title *How to Look Elegant and Impress a Gentleman*.

Lottie waved her arms and pointed at the carrot sticks. "Lady Eggley loves carrots," she whispered. "She must have brought them here on the kitchen cart. I bet Daisy was after them, too!"

Lady Eggley stirred at the sound of Lottie's whisper and muttered something in her sleep again.

Ella felt a fluttering in her tummy. If Lady Eggley woke up now, she'd take them straight to the Headmistress!

Quickly, she reached over and took all the carrots off the plate. Daisy, who had nearly reached the vegetables, looked at her reproachfully. Crouching back down, Ella held the carrots close to the floor and edged backward. After a moment, the little rabbit jumped down from the bedside table and followed the carrots.

Ella crawled backward, holding the carrots out in front of her. She kept her eyes fixed on Daisy. Lottie tried to step out of Ella's way and bumped into the dresser, making it rattle.

Lady Eggley jerked in the bed. "The princesses forgot to curtsy? Someone must be punished!"

Ella's heart pounded so loud she wondered for a moment if everyone would hear it. Then the teacher dozed off again. Checking that Lottie was out of the way, Ella crept backward with the carrots. Daisy hopped after her with her nose twitching. At last they reached the corridor and Ella gently picked up Daisy and hugged her tight. "Silly thing!" she murmured. "I was so worried about you."

Daisy twitched her nose. Then she took a carrot stick from Ella's hand and crunched it.

The princesses took Daisy upstairs to Seahorse Tower. They knew that the main doors of the castle were locked at night and they'd have to wait until morning to take the baby rabbit back to the pet barn. Ella didn't really mind. It gave her a chance for a longer cuddle with her bunny. She pressed her cheek against Daisy's warm fur, glad that the baby animal was safe.

Summer found a small, empty suitcase and padded it with a wooly scarf to make a comfortable sleeping place for Daisy.

"What a strange adventure!" Summer yawned. "It was amazing how that little golden shell opened up a whole secret passageway."

Lottie's eyes gleamed. "Maybe there are other golden shells hidden around the castle that will take us into more tunnels."

"Well, I'm definitely too tired to look for them tonight," said Rosalind. "My legs are aching. I feel like I've walked for miles and miles!"

"Me too," agreed Ella. "I'm really looking forward to getting into bed! I bet even Daisy's tired."

They all looked over at the baby rabbit snuggled up among the folds of the wooly scarf and saw that she'd fallen fast asleep.

CHAPTER TWELVE

Pet Picnic Day

In the morning, the four princesses got dressed early before the rest of Seahorse Tower was awake and took Daisy down to the pet barn.

Ella kissed the rabbit's floppy ears before placing her back in the hutch with her brothers and sisters. She got some extra hay for the rabbits and helped Rebecca move the hay bales into another part of the barn. Daisy hopped up and down her run happily with her ears pricked up.

"She's still got lots of energy, even after hopping down all those passageways," said Lottie, smiling.

"She's quite an adventurous rabbit," said Ella.

"Hey — you know what today is?" said Rosalind, suddenly excited. "It's Pet Picnic Day!"

"Ooh, yes!" said Summer. "I'd forgotten about that."

"What's Pet Picnic Day?" asked Ella.

"Every month we have a picnic, and the pets come along, too." Rosalind grinned. "And we're allowed to wear our own clothes instead of the school uniform."

"And the cooks give us the yummiest cakes and cookies for the picnic," added Summer.

"But the best part is that each tower

takes turns at being in charge, and today it's Seahorse Tower's turn!" said Lottie.

A shadow fell in the doorway. "Well, *you* four aren't going to take part in it!" said Molly. "I told Miss Goldwin that you weren't in your room at bedtime last night. She's coming here right now to yell at you."

Ella's stomach turned over. Then she noticed Molly's mean smile and knew she had to say something. "I'm *really* sorry I knocked you over into the water that time," she said to the older girl. "But it was an accident, and I don't think it's fair for you to keep being angry about it."

"Well said!" Rosalind folded her arms and glared at Molly.

"I know that captains are supposed to make sure people follow the rules," added Ella. "But aren't they also supposed to look after new princesses and help them feel at home at Harebell Castle?"

"Yes, Ella," said Miss Goldwin, stepping into the pet barn. "That's *exactly* what they're supposed to do." She gazed at the girls with bright eyes. "As it happens, Rebecca has told me how helpful you've been here in the pet barn. Was there a good reason for you to be out of bed last night?"

"Yes, Miss Goldwin. There was," said Ella truthfully.

The Headmistress turned to the older girl. "You see, Molly. There was no need to worry. But perhaps you'd like to come back to my office where we can talk about your job as a Seahorse Captain."

Molly turned red and muttered, "Yes, Miss Goldwin." Then she left the barn without looking at Ella and the others.

Miss Goldwin smiled. "Now, since it's Pet Picnic Day, you'd better start taking these animals outside. I'm sure the rest

of your tower will be along soon to
help you."

"Yes, Miss Goldwin," said the girls.

The four princesses picked up the
rabbits one by one and put them in a run
on the grass. Then they rushed inside to
get changed into their best dresses for the
picnic.

Ella put on her beautiful cream-
colored dress decorated with green
leaf patterns. She added her favorite
bracelets and a tiara with gleaming gold
flowers.

Rosalind was wearing a dark blue dress
and a golden tiara that sparkled with
sapphires. "I like your bracelets," she told
Ella. "They're really pretty."

"Thanks!" Ella smiled.

Lottie pulled on a crimson dress with
silk sleeves. Then she squashed a ruby
tiara on top of her red curls. "We'd better

hurry. We don't want to let the other girls from our tower do all the work."

"I'm almost ready!" Summer smoothed her dress, which was edged with red ribbon. Then she quickly brushed her golden hair.

The princesses rushed down to the kitchen, where they collected a bundle of picnic blankets and three large baskets. The baskets were filled with sandwiches, pigs-in-a-blanket, and the biggest chocolate cake Ella had ever seen.

They took everything out to the field and began spreading the picnic blankets on the grass. They handed out plates decorated with a starfish pattern and poured glasses of sparkling lemonade for everyone.

The whole school sat down on the picnic blankets to enjoy lunch while their pets played around them. Ella took a bite of delicious chocolate cake. She could see

Daisy bouncing up and down, enjoying the fresh air and the warm sunshine.

Lottie's sister, Emily, and her friends from Coral Tower came to sit with Ella and the others. One girl, Freya, was holding a lovely black cat with blue eyes and white paws.

Freya shook back her blond braids and said to Lottie, "Do you remember my kitten, Minky? You were staying at my castle in Northernland when Minky got lost in the snow."

"Of course I remember!" said Lottie, stroking the little black cat. "I could never forget you, Minky."

After the picnic, Miss Goldwin organized them into teams for a three-legged race and a beanbag toss.

Lottie's pony, Strawberry, trotted up to the fence to find out what all the excitement was about. He shook his long mane and whinnied. Then Summer's parrot flew down to perch on her shoulder, not wanting to miss out on the fun either.

Ella picked up Daisy from her rabbit run and hugged her. She looked around at all the girls and their pets having fun together. The castle looked bright in the sunshine. A gentle breeze blew in from the cliffs where the orange-and-white lighthouse gleamed in the middle of a sparkling blue sea.

"Are you all right, Ella?" asked Rosalind.

"I'm so glad I came here," Ella told her with a big smile. "I know I'm going to love being a Rescue Princess."

The Rescue Princesses

See how it all began!

The Secret Promise

Read about how Lottie's big sister Emily started the Rescue Princesses in this special sneak peek!

Emily ran between the trees, glad that the other princesses were beside her.

It was much darker out here beyond the castle walls. Low branches reached down to catch them and Emily had to stop and untangle herself.

"Do you think we're going the right way?" she asked.

"Listen," said Clarabel. "I think I heard it again."

They stopped for a moment, trying to hear the animal noise over the wind blowing and the swooshing of the leaves.

"There it is," said Lulu.

The half-crying, half-grunting noise sounded much weaker now. The princesses ran toward it, slowing down as the ground became thick with tree roots and brambles.

On the earth lay a young deer with one leg bent at an awkward angle. The animal turned its black eyes on them, trembling with fright. Emily caught the glint of something silver on the ground.

"Look! It's caught in something," she said.

Clarabel knelt down next to the deer. "Poor thing! No wonder it made that horrible noise."

"That looks like a man-made trap," said Jaminta grimly.

"Why would anyone trap an animal like this?" said Clarabel. "I'm sure it's not allowed."

"King Gudland doesn't seem like the sort of king who would let this happen," agreed Emily. "How are we going to set it free?"

Jaminta bent down to look more closely at the metal teeth of the trap. The emeralds on her wrist cast a bright-green light over everything. Clarabel spoke soothingly to the deer, trying to calm down the shivering animal.

"The trap's clamped really tightly around its foot. It won't be easy to release it," said Jaminta. "Even if we manage to open it, the deer still won't be able to walk."

"Just get that trap open!" said Lulu. "I've got an idea." She turned and sprinted away through the forest.

Jaminta pulled a small screwdriver out of her dress pocket. "Could you keep its leg really still?" she said to Emily.

Emily nodded and held on to the deer's leg firmly, its brown coat feeling velvety beneath her hands. The creature quivered, its huge black eyes opening wide with fear.

"Don't worry," whispered Clarabel, stroking between its ears. "We'll have you free in no time." The young animal turned its soft nose toward her and its ears twitched. It almost seemed as if it knew what she was saying.

Jaminta worked quickly, loosening four screws on the trap, one after the other. The deer squirmed and Emily struggled to keep it still. She kept a tight hold on the leg, praying that Jaminta could work magic with her screwdriver and get the trap undone.

"Stay still, little one," murmured Clarabel.

Jaminta twisted the screws looser, one by one. "Almost there," she said.

The deer wriggled harder, and for a moment Emily thought she would lose her grip on its leg.

"That's it!" Jaminta pulled out the last screw and stuck the screwdriver behind her ear.

Emily pulled the trap open, keeping her fingers away from its sharp silver teeth. Gently she lifted out the deer's leg.

"Look! There's no cut here at all," she said. "Maybe this little deer just fell badly when the trap closed."

"Luckily, it's young and its small leg fit right between the teeth of the trap. Otherwise its injuries would have been much worse," said Jaminta.

Puppy Powers

Get your paws on the Puppy Powers series!

There's something special about the animals at Power's Pets ... something downright magical!